Safety

By Elsie Nelley

Contents

Keeping Food Safe

Food poisoning is very unpleasant. However, it can be prevented if people understand how to handle food safely.

Hygiene

A high standard of hygiene will prevent bacteria from spreading.

People should realise that it is important to wash their hands thoroughly with soap and water before preparing or handling any food. They should then dry their hands on a clean towel.

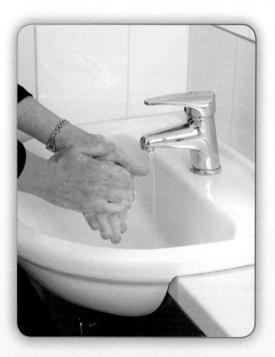
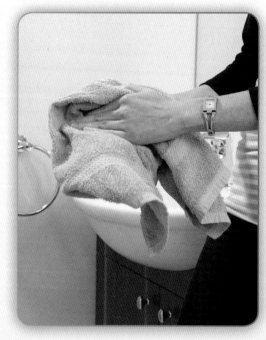

This procedure must be repeated when preparing different foods, especially after handling raw meat, fish or poultry.

Bench surfaces, chopping boards, knives and other utensils must be cleaned each time they have been used.

Refrigeration

Leaving food for any length of time at room temperature can encourage harmful bacteria to grow. Meat, fish and poultry must be refrigerated until it is time to cook them.

Frozen foods need to be thoroughly defrosted before cooking to make sure they are safe to eat.

Cooking

If possible, meat and poultry should be precooked before being grilled on a barbecue. Foods that are grilled can appear cooked on the outside. However, they may not have been cooked for long enough, or cooked at high enough temperatures, to kill bacteria on the inside.

When eating outdoors, keep all food covered until it is ready to be cooked or eaten.

Leftover foods need to be reheated until they are steaming hot. They should never be reheated more than once.

Storage

Cover all food with cling wrap or place in a clean air-tight container before storing. This reduces the possibility of bacteria spreading from one food to another.

Always remember to place uncooked meat and poultry on the bottom shelf of the refrigerator so they do not touch or drip onto other food.

Food should be sealed correctly and placed in the refrigerator or freezer immediately.

Make sure foods that need to be kept cool are stored at the proper temperature to prevent or slow the growth of bacteria.

Leftover foods should be cooled as quickly as possible before being stored in a clean refrigerator or freezer.

Ready-to-eat cooked meats bought from the supermarket need to be kept in a refrigerator until they are eaten.

When food is handled safely, food poisoning is less likely to occur.

The Farmers' Market

Many people in our town prefer to do their weekend shopping at the Green Bay Farmers' Market. The produce is locally grown and always fresh.

The fruit and vegetable stalls are well organised and attractively displayed. Gazebos and large sun shades are erected over these stalls early in the morning. This protects the produce from the Sun throughout the day.

Organically grown seasonal fruit and vegetables have become more and more important in recent years, as people prefer to eat produce that does not contain chemicals such as pesticides.

Organic products available at the market are clearly labelled and small slices of fruit are often arranged on covered platters. People are encouraged to sample a piece of fruit even if they don't intend to buy any.

Free-range eggs are sold at the market. They come from farms where the hens wander freely, eating insects, grubs and vegetation. The hens usually lay their eggs on fresh straw in boxes inside a hen house.

The eggs at this stall are always clean; they do not have feathers or dirt stuck to the shells. They are displayed on trays so customers can see they are not cracked or broken.

Large awnings keep bakery stalls shaded and cool. The bakers wear clean aprons and disposable gloves, which they change regularly for new ones. The gloves prevent their bare hands from coming into contact with any food.

Before arriving at the market, the bakers prepare a variety of breads, cakes and biscuits. The goods are then displayed in clean containers and are clearly labelled for customers. The bakers use tongs to place items into paper bags.

Stall holders at the Green Bay Farmers' Market understand the importance of strict food safety rules. People who do their weekend shopping at the market know they are purchasing the very best local produce.